MEL BAY PRESENTS

David Barrett's Harmonica
Blues Harmonica Jam Tracks & Soloing Concepts #2

LEVEL 2
COMPLETE BLUES HARMONICA LESSON SERIES

ONLINE AUDIO

1. Intro Music [:47]
2. A Word From the Author [1:10]
3. Section 1 – Notation [:17]
4. Section 2 – What is Blues? [3:35]
5. Section 3 – Opening Licks Exercise 3.1-3.3 [2:17]
6. Exercise 3.4 [1:47]
7. Exercise 3.5 [1:16]
8. Breaks Exercise 3.6 [:53]
9. Endings Exercise 3.10 [1:30]
10. Section 4 – Phrasing Level I [1:15]
11. Contrast Exercise 4.1 [:55]
12. 24 Measure Solo [1:22]
13. Organizing a Song [:59]
14. Head Exercise 4.3 [:40]
15. Opening Exercise 4.4 [:43]
16. Soloing Blocks [1:20]
17. 1st - 3rd Hole Soloing Block Exercise 4.6 [1:40]
18. Chord Tone Soling Exercise 4.7 [1:01]
19. Example Song Using 1st - 3rd Hole Soloing Block [:48]
20. Example Song Using 1st - 3rd Hole Soloing Block Exercise 4.8 [2:21]
21. Breakdown on all that just happened [:36]
22. 1st - 4th Hole Soloing Block [:37]
23. Exercise 4.9 - 4.10 [:24]
24. Overview [:45]
25. Section 5 – Intro [2:04]
26. Section 6 – Big Boy's Jam [2:37]
27. Section 7 [1:17]
28. 12 Bar Jam #1 [2:27]
29. 12 Bar Jam #2 [2:22]
30. 12 Bar Jam #3 [4:43]
31. 12 Bar Jam #4 [3:41]
32. 12 Bar Jam #5 [2:46]
33. 12 Bar Jam #6 [3:45]
34. 12 Bar Jam #7 [3:28]
35. 12 Bar Jam #8 [4:44]
36. 12 Bar Jam #9 [2:48]

To Access the Online Audio Go To:
www.melbay.com/99110BCDEB

Visit us on the Web at www.melbay.com — E-mail us at email@melbay.com

1 2 3 4 5 6 7 8 9 0

Contents

Thanks to John Scerbo and Mark Fenichel for proof reading.
Also, to my wife Nozomi and our family for their never-ending support.

A Word from the Author

Welcome to *Harmonica Masterclass Complete Blues Harmonica Lesson Series Level Two*. My name is David Barrett, and I'm the author of this lesson series. At this level you should have already studied the book and CD *Basic Blues Harmonica Method, Basic Blues Harmonica Method Video,* and *Blues Harmonica Jam Tracks & Soloing Concepts #1.* You should now be studying *Classic Chicago Blues Harp* w/CD *#1, Building Harmonica Technique Videos #1 and #2,* and *Scales, Patterns & Bending Exercises #1.* Although the book/CD combination can stand on its own, the studies found within the materials in this series (and the previous series) will help you tremendously in understanding the ideas talked about in this book. Refer to the back of this book for details about the entire *Harmonica Masterclass* series. If you have any questions regarding this book, or any other books within the line, look at the Harmonica Masterclass web-site at www.harmonicamasterclass.com, or contact us by mail at PO Box 1723, Morgan Hill, CA 95038. Good luck and have fun!

Section 1 - A Word about Notation

The harmonica notation in this booklet is based on the ten hole diatonic harmonica played in 2nd position. You are using 2nd position when you play in a key exactly five scale degrees higher than that in which the harmonica is tuned (e.g., you would play a "C" major harmonica in the key of "G" major).

Harmonica players use a wide variety of keyed harmonicas in their music. For ease of reading, all harmonica parts played on the ten hole diatonic harmonica will use the key signature of C major. This will put you in the pitch set of a C major harmonica. Through years of teaching, transcribing, and writing music books with Mel Bay Publications, I have found this method of notation to be the fastest for translating musical thought. Diagrammed below is a C major ten hole diatonic harmonica.

BLOW →	C	E	G	C	E	G	C	E	G	C
C	1	2	3	4	5	6	7	8	9	10
DRAW →	D	G	B	D	F	A	B	D	F	A

Harmonica Tablature

You will notice in the diagram that each hole has a corresponding number. In the tablature, the number corresponding to the hole will be under the notational symbol for the note to be played. When a note stands by itself, the note is to be drawn upon (inhaled.) When a number is followed with a plus (+), the note is to be blown (exhaled.) If the note is to be bent, a series of slashes will be notated to the right of the number. Each slash represents a half-step bend. For example: three draw (3), bent down a half step, would be "B-flat" and would be notated as 3'. Three draw, bent down a whole-step, would be "A" and would be notated as 3". Three draw, bent down a whole-step and one-half (minor third bend,) would be "A-flat" and would be notated as 3'''. Diagrammed on the next page is the entire bend chart for a C major diatonic harmonica.

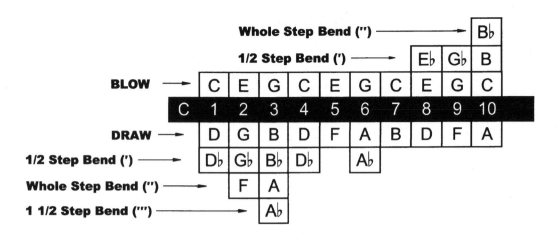

Whole Step Bend (")											Bb
1/2 Step Bend (')									Eb	Gb	B
BLOW →	C	E	G	C	E	G	C	E	G	C
C	1	2	3	4	5	6	7	8	9	10
DRAW →	D	G	B	D	F	A	B	D	F	A
1/2 Step Bend (') →	Db	Gb	Bb	Db		Ab				
Whole Step Bend (") →		F	A							
1 1/2 Step Bend (''') →			Ab							

Rhythm

The rhythmic notation used is based on classical notational norms with the exception of the swinging of rhythms. Most rhythmic patterns played by a blues musician are swung. The word *Swing* means to take an eighth note pattern that would otherwise be played straight (1/2 & 1/2 = 1) and elongates the first eighth (2/3) while shortening and placing the second eighth later in time relative to the first eighth (1/3) (2/3 & 1/3 = 1.) If the notation showed every part that is swung, instead of seeing two eighth notes together you would see three triplet-eighths with the first two notes in the triplet figure tied together. This would crowd the music very quickly and make it very difficult to read. You will not see any markers indicating that a rhythm is swung. As in jazz, swing is always assumed.

Notation That is Specific to Harmonica Tablature

Written below are some symbols that might be foreign to you. Some symbols are specific to my notational style. I think you will find them useful.

Ex. 1.1 - The Two Hole Shake

Ex. 1.1 - The **Two-Hole Shake** is achieved by sliding your lips between two holes on the harmonica. These holes can be any combination of adjacent holes. When this notation is used in octaves, the flutter-tongue is used in place of the two-hole shake.

Ex. 1.2 - The Dip Bend

Ex. 1.2 - The **Dip Bend** is a way of notating an upward bend that would normally be too fast to fully notate. Start the note in the bend, then release to the natural note.

Ex. 1.3 - The Pull

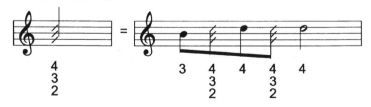

Ex. 1.3 - The **Pull** is a percussive technique usually used on the up beat to create a syncopated rhythmic feel. Placing the tongue over every hole in your embouchure (2 to 5 holes,) and releasing the tongue to get a very short articulate chord performs the pull. Slashes are used as the note heads for the notes of the pull.

Ex. 1.4 - Tongue Block

Ex. 1.4 - The **Tongue Block** symbol is used when the artist uses a tongue slap. When tongue blocking a single hole you place your mouth over three holes and block the two holes to the left, leaving the hole to the right to sound. The tongue slap is achieved by breathing a split second early (allowing all three reeds to vibrate), then attacking the two holes with your tongue, leaving the right hole open. This gives you the initial thickness of three holes vibrating. When moving the tongue into place, the air that it took to vibrate three reeds is then forced into one, creating a strong attack.

Ex. 1.5 - Staccato

Ex. 1.5 - The **Staccato** notation directs the player to play that note shortly and briskly. The note with the staccato still gets its full rhythmic value; it is the duration that is cut.

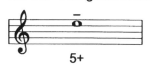
Ex. 1.6 - Elongated Note

Ex. 1.6 - The **Elongated Note** is just what its name implies. The note with this notation will get a longer duration, sometimes making the second note in the passage (if a swing eighth) shorter.

Ex. 1.7 - The **Octave Tongue block** shows that two notes are played at the same time in octaves. When performing an octave you place your mouth over four holes (five on the high draws) and block the middle holes, which causes only the top and bottom notes to be played.

Ex. 1.7 - Octave Tongue Block

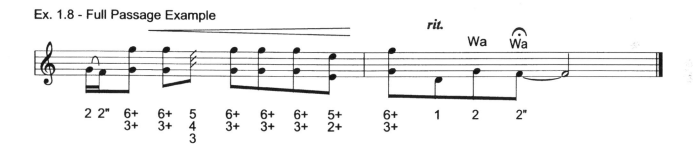
Ex. 1.8 - Full Passage Example

Ex. 1.8 - The above example is taken from track number 4 "Going Down This Highway" from my transcription book of William Clarke's CD "Serious Intentions." On the left, over the 2-draw and 2" whole-step bend, is a **Slur**. A slur is a curved line that indicates that there is to be no break between the two notes. A little to the right and above the notes, is a long double line which opens as it reaches the next measure. This is a **Crescendo**. A crescendo is a gradual change in volume. In this case the volume gets louder as the second measure comes nearer. After the crescendo the term *rit.* is written. *Rit* is an abbreviation for **Ritardando**, which means decrease the tempo until the piece finishes. Use of the ritardando gives a passage a more dramatic ending. To the right of the ritardando is a small marking that says **Wa**. This notation is used to direct the player to start from a closed hand position (the cup) and then open up before the note is finished. The last notation example is the **Fermata**. The fermata, usually placed at the end of a phrase or song, is used to notate that the note or chord it is placed above is held indeterminately until the bandleader directs the music to stop.

Section 2 – What Is Blues?

Here is a quick review of 12 bar blues from book one. The standard length of a blues progression is 12 measures long, using only three chords for its structure. This 12 bar progression is repeated until the song ends. Musicians add variety by playing with the voicing of the chords and by adding small riffs, called hooks, to add interest and unification to a song. The best aspect of blues for the soloist is that the background progression is simple. This allows the soloist much time to explore and develop solos. To look further into 12 bar blues we need to know a bit more about chords, which are based on the scale of the key of the piece. Example 2.1 is the C major scale.

Ex. 2.1

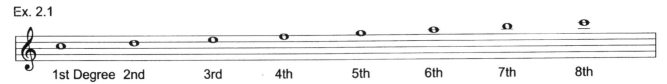

1st Degree   2nd   3rd   4th   5th   6th   7th   8th

A chord can be built upon each scale degree. A **Chord** is a vertical structure created when three or more notes are struck simultaneously (all at the same time) or arpeggiated (one right after the other) in thirds. For example: If you strike the first, third, and fifth scale degree at the same time you will get a I* (one) chord. If you strike the second, fourth, and sixth scale degrees at the same time you will get a ii chord. There are seven chords possible in any given key. Diagrammed below are all the chords available.

Ex. 2.2

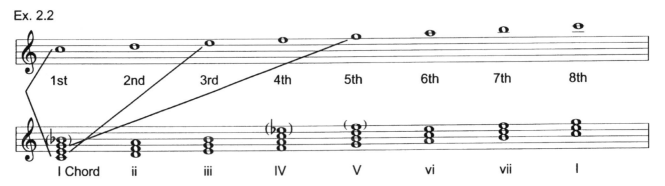

1st   2nd   3rd   4th   5th   6th   7th   8th

I Chord   ii   iii   IV   V   vi   vii   I

Blues uses the One Chord (I), Four Chord (IV), and Five Chord (V) from this set. On top of these chords a flatted-3rd is added to make a Dominant-7th chord. Demonstrated below is the standard 12 bar blues progression.

Ex. 2.3

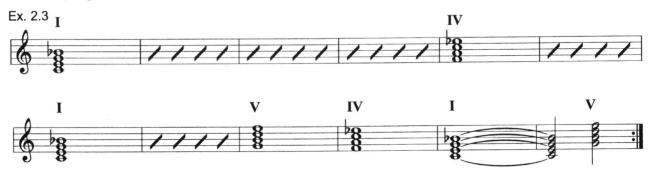

*Roman numerals, as opposed to the actual note name of the chord (C chord, G chord, etc,) will be used to designate the chords. Roman numerals are used as functions, thus allowing you talk broadly about a chord function without restricting yourself to a key. Upper-case roman numerals indicate a major chord and lower case roman numerals indicate a minor chord.

Section 3 – **Form Elements**

In the last book we studied how to construct the individual components of a 12 bar solo. Within this book we will study how to construct and solo over an entire blues song. Let's start by looking at how a song starts and ends.

There are many ways to start a blues song. Most commonly the start is depicted by the chord of the 12 bar blues progression on which you start. When you or a band member says you are "starting on the **I**" or "from the top," it means that you are to start on the **I** chord at the beginning of the 12 bar blues progression. The start can be signaled by a verbal count-off; a tapping of drum sticks for four beats; a bouncing gesture in a four count on a guitar neck; or one simple lift of the body and movement back down from the band leader. Example 3.1 demonstrates this below.

Another way to begin a song is by "starting on the **V**." This starts the song on the 9th measure at the start of the **V-IV-I** Transition. Example 3.2 below demonstrates this.

The example below demonstrates the use of the harmonica by itself to start the song. This is a very effective way of telling the listener which instrument is most important in this song. This example shows the harmonica part starting on the **I** and the band coming in on the **IV**.

Ex. 3.3 - C Harmonica

This second example has the harmonica playing the entire opening 12 measures by itself. This opening is particularly effective in a jam situation with musicians you have never played with before. It s hard to convey to the band with words the feel of the song you want to play. By playing a bass-like line in the opening, you are telling the bass player what he or she is supposed to play when the band comes in. If the song also has a hook or rhythmic figure, play that hook as soon as the band comes in so that the guitarist or other solo instrument, such as sax, can hear that this is the theme of the song. Now that you have given everybody his or her part, you can start your solo.

Ex. 3.4 - D Harmonica

This line is what the bass player will take over after this 12 bar opening.

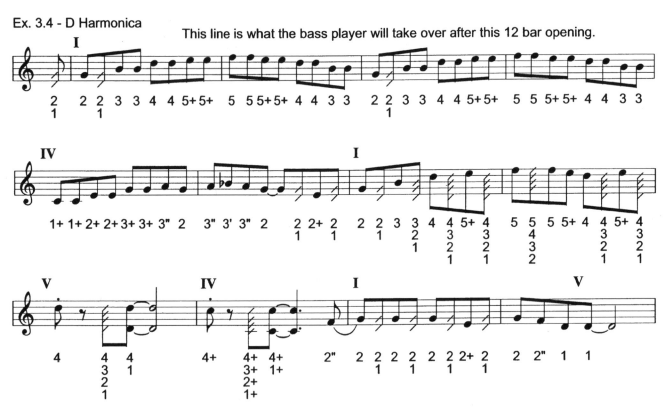

The first measure is the hook. The second measure is the rhythmic figure that you want the drums and rhythm guitar to play.

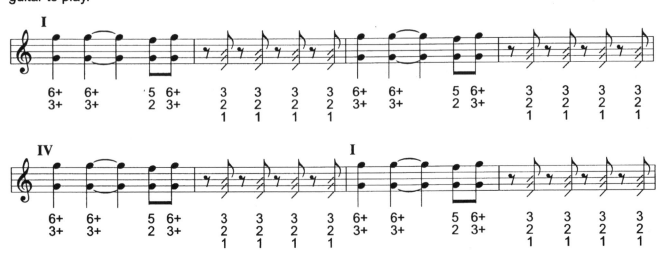

Breaks are used to add variety to a song. A break is a place where the band stops and restarts in a repeated pattern. The break leaves a space for you to play. Demonstrated below is a common use of the break. This example uses two measure breaks on the first four measures leading into the IV chord, making it a 16 bar blues. It is also very common to play one measure breaks. The harmonica will play both the break and the solo part. The break is encased in brackets.

Ex. 3.5 - C Harmonica

If you are the soloist, the band plays the notes of the break as your rest until the hole where you solo. If you are not the soloist you will play the breaks with the band. Detailed on the next page are the most common harmonica lines used for a break. Any line can pretty much be used as long as it starts on the "and" (upbeat) of the 3rd beat and finishes on the downbeat of the next measure.

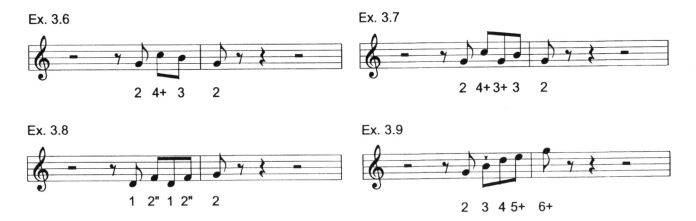

Ex. 3.6

2 4+ 3   2

Ex. 3.7

2 4+3+ 3   2

Ex. 3.8

1 2" 1 2"   2

Ex. 3.9

2 3 4 5+ 6+

The break can also be played throughout an entire 12 bar section, or even as short as just on the **IV** chord of the **V-IV-I** Transition. The break is a great way to add variety to a song and can be placed almost anywhere. Listen to these songs for great examples of the break: *I'm Ready* from *Classic Chicago Blues Harp Book #1* by Mary Johnson; *I'm A Man* by Ellas McDaniel (Bo Diddley); and *Don't Start Me Talkin'* by Sonny Boy Williamson II (Rice Miller.)

There are as many choices to end a song as there are to begin one. The most common way to end a song is detailed below. You will find this example to be a universal ending that any blues musician knows how to play.

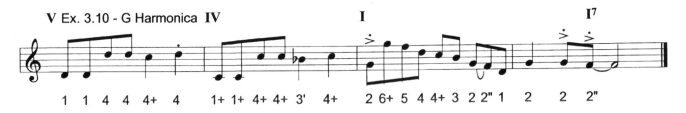

V Ex. 3.10 - G Harmonica **IV**   **I**   **I⁷**

1 1 4 4 4+ 4   1+ 1+ 4+ 4+ 3' 4+   2 6+ 5 4 4+ 3 2 2" 1 2   2   2"

For the above example, you heard the band stop on the downbeat of the **I** chord after the **V-IV-I** Transition; this hit is notated with an accent mark. The band then returns on the 2nd beat of the 12th measure; these two hits are also notated with an accent mark. The 2nd beat in measure 12 is a **I** chord and the "and" (upbeat) of the 2nd beat is a **I⁷** chord. Even though the band is usually playing 7th chords throughout the song, at the end, the 7th is emphasized strongly. Your two most common notes to end on would be this 7th or the root.

Another type of ending used very often by the performer Paul Butterfield is to start the break on the **IV** chord. Detailed below is an example of this.

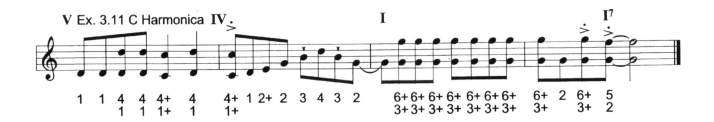

V Ex. 3.11 C Harmonica **IV**   **I**   **I⁷**

1 1 4 4 4+ 4   4+ 1 2+ 2 3 4 3 2   6+ 6+ 6+ 6+ 6+ 6+ 6+   6+ 2 6+   5
1 1 1+ 1   1+   3+ 3+ 3+ 3+ 3+ 3+ 3+   3+   3+   2

Section 4 – **Phrasing Level 2**

Now that we know the phrasing within 12 bar blues and the song elements used within a blues song, it's time to build your solo. The chart below demonstrates the flow of thought through a 12 bar solo. The key here is to see the importance of the first lick. Look at how the first lick dictates what follows.

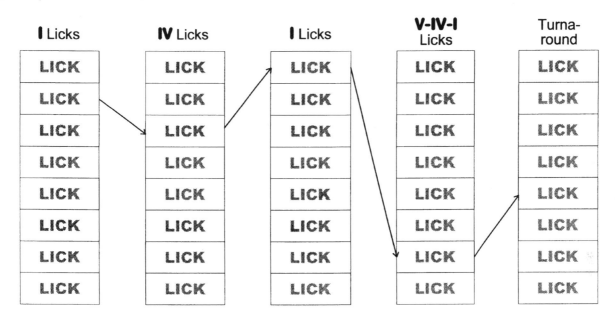

I Licks	**IV** Licks	**I** Licks	**V-IV-I** Licks	Turna-round
LICK	LICK	LICK	LICK	LICK
LICK	LICK	LICK	LICK	LICK
LICK	LICK	LICK	LICK	LICK
LICK	LICK	LICK	LICK	LICK
LICK	LICK	LICK	LICK	LICK
LICK	LICK	LICK	LICK	LICK
LICK	LICK	LICK	LICK	LICK
LICK	LICK	LICK	LICK	LICK

Organizing A Solo

When organizing your solo, you want to think about a couple things before you begin. Think of the form elements that make the song unique. If the song has a strong hook or melody throughout, you will want to include parts of these elements in your solo, either in actual parts of the line or the emphasis of rhythm. If the song has a major feel, emphasize the more major notes and stay away from the notes within the blues scale. If the song is very bluesy, you will want to emphasize notes within the blues scale, and you probably want to emphasize thick textures that are created by two note combinations such as the 4 draw and 5 draw together. Again, think of the form elements that make the song unique. Your goal is to add to the compositional aspects of the song by emulating the traits of the song in your soloing and background.

Contrast is probably your most important tool as a soloist. Your solo will become very stagnant if you don't have a plan in mind for where your solo is leading. I'm sure you are, or have been, in a rut where all of your solos start sounding the same. We all have been there, and will go there time-and-time-again throughout our evolution as soloists.

Let's now look at a couple of different length solos to get a feel for how to chain phrases together. Before we go into a solo longer than 12 bars, I want to show you what I meant by contrast. Look at how the **IV** chord is treated in example 4.1. The **I** chord licks are very active, sweeping across the entire harmonica. The **IV** chord is a total contrast to this by just sitting on the 2 draw. This is what is meant by contrast.

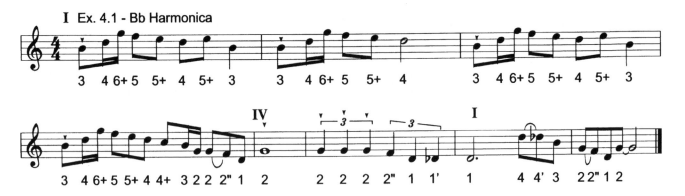

The example below is a 24 measure solo. Look at how the 1st solo only emphasizes the 1st through 4th holes. The 2nd solo then emphasizes the 4th through 6th holes with octaves. This simple separation is plenty to add contrast between the two solos.

Organizing A Song

A solo three verses or longer works differently than the shorter one to two verse solos. It's time to not just play good sounding riffs that emphasize different parts of the harmonica; we need to take each solo and build it to the next, and take the listener on a journey. Our next step is to construct an entire instrumental piece. When writing a piece of music you first need to think of how you can make this new song unique. The **Head** is the theme of your composition. The head should be something catchy but not too complex. Your goal is to have your listeners go home humming your song. The head is stated in the beginning of a song and then repeated at the close of the song. In longer instrumentals where many instruments solo, the head can be repeated throughout the song to add a unifying theme. For this section we will use the song *Big Boy's Jam* from the Book *Building Harmonica Technique* written by me and published by Mel Bay Publications. Detailed below is the head from the song. When listening to the song in its entirety, notice how the head sticks out, more due to its rhythm than the notes used. The open circles above the note heads denote the use of the tongue block.

For this piece I've added an opening to grab the attention of the listener. You usually don't want a strong solo on the first verse; it doesn't leave you with anything to build upon. For this piece it works O.K. Notice in measure five I use a half-step bend marking on the 5 draw. Keep in mind that this 5 draw bend does not bend down an entire half-step, it can only bend down a quarter-tone. This half-step marking is used in this case to indicate the use of the bend. The note is notated as an F-flat with a plus above the note. The plus denotes that it is an F-flat plus a quarter-tone. Detailed below is the opening to the song.

Before moving further into the song I need to show you a soloing technique. Many years ago the player Gary Smith showed me (he told me Charlie Musselwhite showed him) "masking the harp." The idea behind masking the harp is to select an area on the harmonica such as the 1st through 3rd hole and cover up (mentally or physically) the remaining holes of the harmonica. We will use the term **Soloing Block**. If you were to pick the 1st through 3rd hole soloing block you would only play the notes found within the 1st through 3rd hole. For a given period of time (usually three weeks of practice every day for one soloing block) you will only play that soloing block. A list of benefits from the use of this technique are detailed below.

Merits of the technique Soloing Blocks:
1. Due to the limitation of pitches, your ability to construct phrases becomes stronger. If you play with no plan in mind, you will start repeating yourself as soon as the second verse.

2. Your bending becomes more articulate. As you will see, bending will give you many more notes to work with in your soloing block. To make use of the bends you will need to strengthen your ability to move in and out of the bends with accuracy.
3. You gain a stronger understanding of that portion of the harmonica. After studying soloing blocks you will be able to go to any part of your harmonica and solo confidently knowing that you can stay there as long as you want.

Let's start by looking at the 1st through 3rd hole soloing block. Detailed below is a list of questions we need to ask ourselves so that we can understand our first soloing block better before starting.

1. *How many notes are available?*
2. *Where are the root notes for each chord?*
3. *Where are all of the chord tones?*
4. *What techniques are available?*
5. *What makes this soloing block good?*

1st through 3rd Hole Soloing Book

How many notes are available?
For the 1st through 3rd holes we have twelve notes available. Wow! Twelve notes available for just three holes. Look at the diagram below to see the note spread for the 1st through 3rd holes.

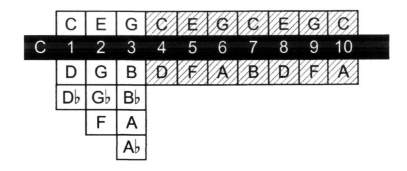

Where are the root notes for each chord?
Your root notes are the notes of most agreement for each chord. For this soloing block the **I** chord roots are on the 2 draw or 3 blow (G); the **IV** chord root is on the 1 blow (C); and the **V** chord root is on the 1 draw (D.) Play the exercise below to get a feel for the 1st thought 3rd hole root notes.

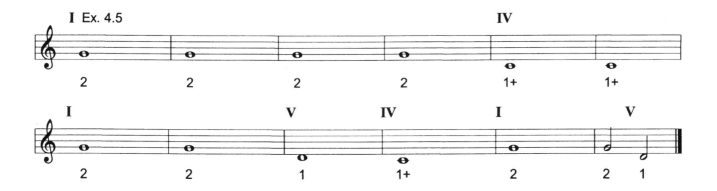

Where are all of the chord tones?

Each note of the chord is a possible place to rest upon in a solo. The chord-tones for the **I**, **IV**, and **V** chord are detailed below. Memorize these notes and what chords they belong to then play example 4.6 below.

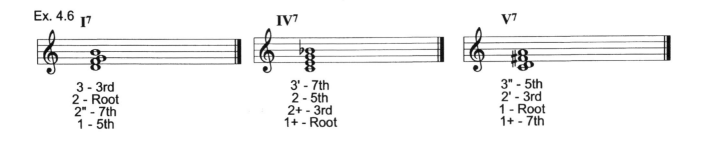

Ex. 4.6 **I**[7]

3 - 3rd
2 - Root
2" - 7th
1 - 5th

IV[7]

3' - 7th
2 - 5th
2+ - 3rd
1+ - Root

V[7]

3" - 5th
2' - 3rd
1 - Root
1+ - 7th

I Ex. 4.7 - D Harmonica

2   3 2 2 2" 1 2"   3 2 2" 1   2"

IV   **I**

1+ 1+ 2+ 3+ 3'   1+ 1+ 2+ 3+ 3'   2 2" 1 2 1   3 2 2" 1 2   2 3 2

V   **IV**   **I**   **V**

3"   3'   2 2 2 2 2 2 2   2   1 1
                                    1   1   1

What techniques are available?

Every technique can be the focus of one of the 12 measure solos. For the 1st through 3rd soloing block we have the: bend; laughing vibrato; bent vibrato on the draw notes; 2/3 draw combination to end a phrase on; chords that comes from the 1-3 draw and 1-3 blow; and tongue slaps.

OK, now that we know all the root notes, chord tones, and have thought of all of the techniques available to us on the 1st through 3rd hole soloing block, let's solo. Remember our goal: to solo as long as we can without sounding repetitive. Think of a theme for every solo and remember to not use all of your notes too soon. Reserve certain notes and combination of notes for later use. Detailed on the next page is a solo that uses the 1st though 3rd soloing block.

Ex. 4.8 - Bb Harmonica

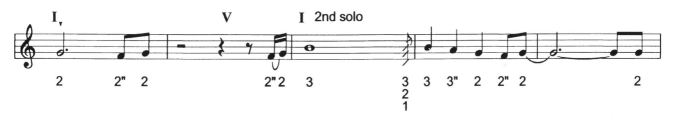

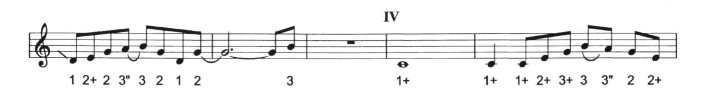

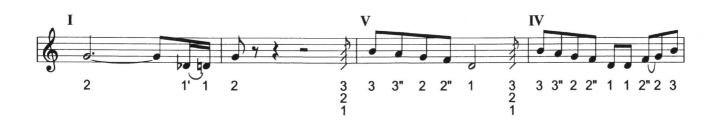

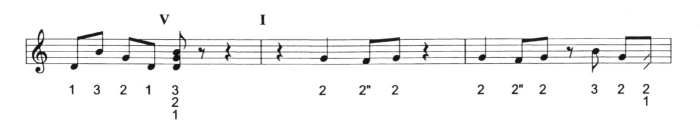

Let's break down what just happened in this last song. The first 12 bar solo starts off very basic following the root notes of each chord. The 2nd solo focuses on the 3 draw. The 3rd solo focuses on the 1 draw. The 4th solo focuses on the 2 draw along with the open chordal sound of the pull on the up-beat. The 5th solo focuses on the 2 whole-step bend (2".) The 6th solo focuses on a rhythmic pattern that arpegiates across all three holes of the soloing block. The 7th solo uses the same notes as the guitarist's hook, creating a type of head. Eighty-four measures... not too bad for only three holes!

1st through 4th Hole Soloing Block

For the 1st through 4th holes we have three more notes available: the 4 blow (C); 4 draw 1/2-step bend (Db); and 4 draw (D.) For this soloing block the **I** chord roots are on the 2 draw or 3 blow (G); the **IV** chord roots are on the 1 blow and 4 blow (C); and the **V** chord roots are on the 1 draw and 4 draw (D.) The **IV** chord and **V** chord root notes can now be played in octaves. Also, jumping between octaves sounds very nice when soloing. Detailed below are the notes available to you between the 1st and 4th holes, and examples 4.9 and 4.10 demonstrating octave movement.

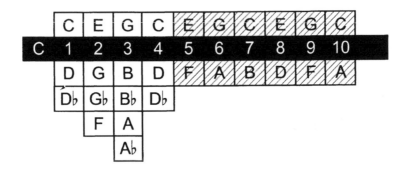

For the 1st through 4th hole soloing block we have a couple more techniques available to us. You have: 1st and 4th hole blow and draw octaves; 3rd and 4th hole draw and blow shakes; tongue slaps and pulls around the 3rd and 4th holes; and most importantly more of the blues scale available.

Other Soloing Blocks

I think you have the idea of soloing blocks now. Use the formula we have used in the last two soloing blocks to research these others. The other soloing blocks are 1st through 5th holes; 1st through 6th holes; and 6th through 10th holes. Again, spend at least three weeks playing within one soloing block. You will be amazed on how many new licks you will create and how good at phrasing you will become.

Section 5 – Soloing Themes

We already know that a head is used in most songs to make the song unique and give it a type of melody the listener can grab on to. We will now look at ideas that help in the construction of an entire instrumental. The template we will use is a song that uses a head in the opening verse and repeats the head at end to bring the song to a close. The numbers in the middle represent 12 bar solo sections. Our goal is to think of ways to solo within this space.

Head	1	2	3	4	5	Head

In most cases a solo starts fairly tamely and builds as it reaches its end. We will do the same. When building in a solo you will: increase in volume; use thicker note combinations; use stronger attack; and play with more intensity. Our first example is a simple one, but one of the most effective ways to build in a solo. Our first theme will be a building of pitch; we will simply start low on the harmonica and build higher on the harmonica as the solo progresses. If you were to start your solo with the 1st through 3rd hole soloing block you could then move to the 1st through 4th hole soloing block for the second verse. The third verse would use the 1st through 5th hole soloing block, building to the 1st through 6th hole soloing block on the fourth verse. The song would then climax using both the high-end and low end of the harmonica. If it where a longer song you could play the 6th through 10th hole soloing block for the fifth verse and then use the entire harmonica for the sixth verse before the head returns. The template below shows this idea.

Head	1	2	3	4	5	Head
	1st – 3rd Holes	1st – 4th Holes	1st – 5th Holes	1st – 6th Holes	Entire Harp	

The song example on the next page is from the book *Building Harmonica Technique* written by me and published by Mel Bay Publications. The song, called *Big Boy's Jam*, is a song that is based on the idea of building in pitch. An opening is used to grab the attention of the listener. The second verse is the head. The third verse uses the 1st through 3rd hole soloing block. The fourth verse uses the 1st through 4th hole soloing block. The fifth verse uses the 1st through 5th hole soloing block. The sixth verse uses the 1st through 6th hole soloing block. The seventh verse uses the entire harmonica. The last verse is the return of the head.

Big Boy's Jam

From the book *Building Harmonica Technique* © 1994 by Mel Bay Publications, Inc.
All Rights Reserved. International Copyright Secured.

24

As you can hear, *Big Boy's Jam* is a great example of how a simple idea can make a great song. Detailed below are more ideas on how you can construct a solo.

Head	1	2	3	4	5	Head
Pitch	1st – 3rd Holes	1st – 4th Holes	1st – 5th Holes	1st – 6th Holes	Entire Harp	
Activity	Short bursts with licks no more than one measure long	Long notes with short endings	Long flowing lines	Chordal passages	Solo that emphasizes thick textures and is intense	
Texture	Single notes	Single note in octaves	Two note combinations such as 3 & 4 and 4 & 5 draw	Tongue slaps	Two hole shakes and thick textures like the 2 & 5 draw octave embouchure	
Pitch/Soloing Block	1st – 3rd Holes	4th – 7th Holes	2nd – 5th Holes	6th – 9th Holes	Entire Harp	
Position Switching	1st Position Low	2nd Position Low	2nd Position Middle Range	3rd Position High	2nd Position Middle Range	

Section 6 – Study Exercises

Listed below are study exercises I have prepared for each section of this book. These are the same exercises I use with my private students; they have proven to be very helpful. There is no answer key in this section since all of the answers can be found in the book.

Study Exercise 1 (Section 3)
1. Listen to ten blues recordings that use harmonica. Listen to how they start and end their songs.
2. Write 3 examples of how you could start a song. Make one of these examples start with the harmonica by itself.
3. Write a 12 bar solo that uses breaks. You will play both the break notes and the solo line.
4. Write three examples of how you could end a song.

Study Exercise 2 (Section 4)
1. Write a 24 measure solo where there is contrast between the first and second solo.
2. Play for three weeks only using the 1st through 3rd hole soloing block.
3. Write a 60 measure (5 verse) solo that only uses the 1st through 3rd hole soloing block. Your goal is to have new and fresh material for each 12 measure verse.
4. Play for three weeks only using the 1st through 4th hole soloing block.
5. Write a 60 measure (5 verse) solo that only uses the 1st through 4th hole soloing block.
6. Play for three weeks only using the 1st through 5th hole soloing block.
7. Write a 60 measure (5 verse) solo that only uses the 1st through 5th hole soloing block.
8. Play for three weeks only using the 6th through 10th hole soloing block.
9. Write a 60 measure (5 verse) solo that only uses the 6th through 10th hole soloing block.

Study Exercise 3 (Section 5)
1. Using the template shown at the beginning of *Section 5* write a song based on the idea of building in pitch as shown in *Big Boy's Jam*.
2. Write one more song based on the ideas shown on page 25, or on an idea of your own.
3. Write an opening solo that will grab the attention of the listener. Write a head. Place a lot of thought into what you are going to use for the head. This is your most important solo. Then think of what your theme will be for the inner solo. Finish the song by repeating the head and using an ending lick.

Section 7 – Blues Harmonica Jam Tracks

The following songs are written by me and performed by the *David Barrett Blues Band* featuring John Garcia on guitar. Some songs with the full band are constructed with a hook. A **hook** is a line that is repeated throughout the song to add unity. The hook can be played by the band over the entire song, such as the songs *Baby Please Don't Go* and *I'm Ready* (found in *Classic Chicago Blues Harp, Series 2.*) The type of hook we are going to use is only played in the opening and ending of the song. The hook will be a small, repeated figure that can be played by any solo instrument, such as the guitar, saxophone or harmonica. Playing this hook will give you a good feel for the song and give you a springboard into other ideas for your solo.

Detailed in this section are charts for each song on the recording. Each chart shows the chords, chord progression, and notes of the hook. Some of the hooks will be notated in octaves. If you are not familiar with octaves just drop the bottom note and only play the top. The harmonica will always be written in 2nd position; the songs can be played in any position. For further understanding of positions move to *Series 3* in the *Harmonica Masterclass*® line.

12 BAR JAM #1

Key of Song: F Major   Tempo: 152   Harmonica: Bb Harmonica in 2nd Position
Song Description: Medium-fast shuffle with Charleston feel   Instrumentation: Full band

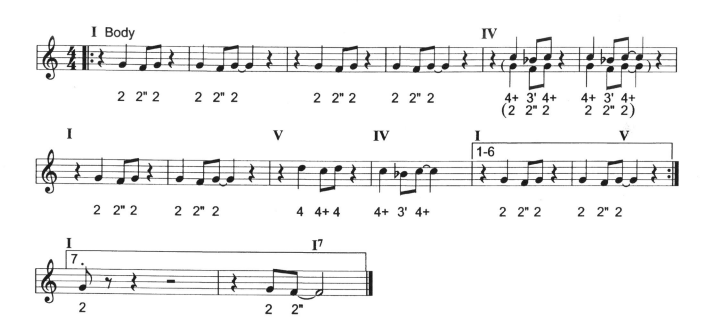

12 BAR JAM #2

Key of Song: A Major   Tempo: 168   Harmonica: D Harmonica in 2nd Position
Song Description: Medium-fast shuffle   Instrumentation: Full band

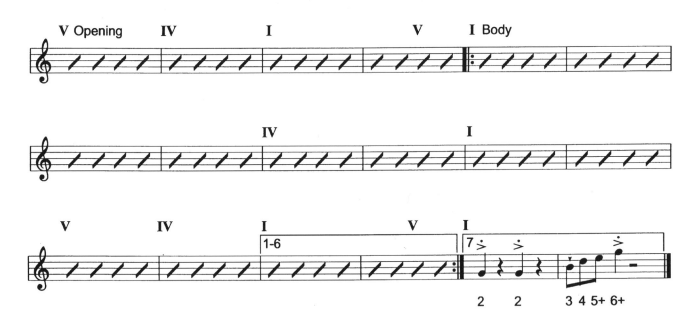

12 BAR JAM #3

Key of Song: A Major   Tempo: 56   Harmonica: D Harmonica in 2nd Position
Song Description: Slow blues   Instrumentation: Full band with only kick on drums

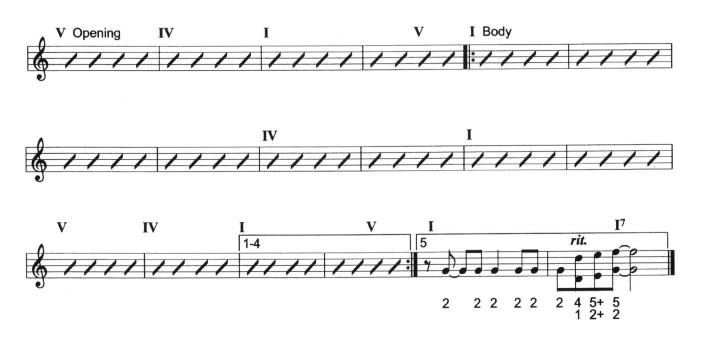

12 BAR JAM #4

<u>Key of Song</u>: F Minor with major feel   <u>Tempo</u>: 100   <u>Harmonica</u>: Bb Harmonica in 2nd Position, Eb
Harmonica in 3rd Position, Lee Oskar F Natural Minor Harmonica in 2nd Position
<u>Song Description</u>: 16 bar medium-fast minor blues with break on **IV**   <u>Instrumentation</u>: Full band

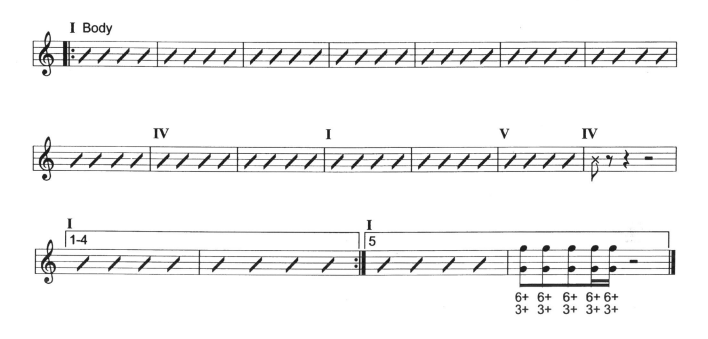

12 BAR JAM #5

<u>Key of Song</u>: Bb Major   <u>Tempo</u>: 192   <u>Harmonica</u>: Eb Harmonica in 2nd Position
<u>Song Description</u>: Fast blues with walking bass   <u>Instrumentation</u>: Full band

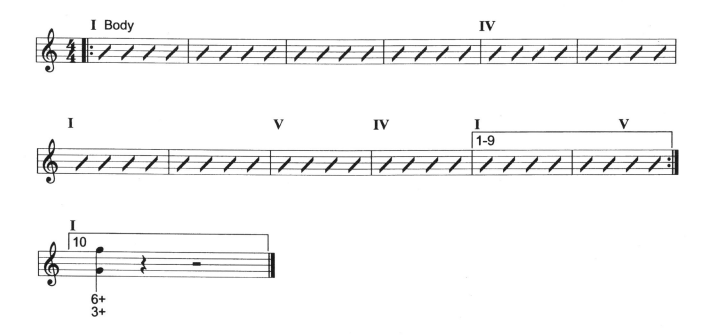

12 BAR JAM #6

Key of Song: D Major   Tempo: 116   Harmonica: G Harmonica in 2nd Position
Song Description: Medium shuffle with slide guitar   Instrumentation: Full band

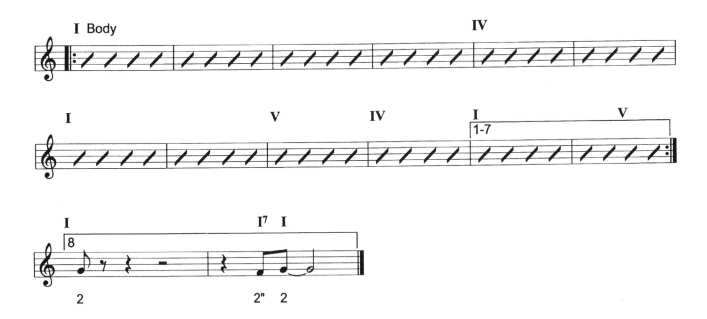

12 BAR JAM #7

Key of Song: G Major   Tempo: 126   Harmonica: C Harmonica in 2nd Position
Song Description: Medium shuffle with breaks   Instrumentation: Full band

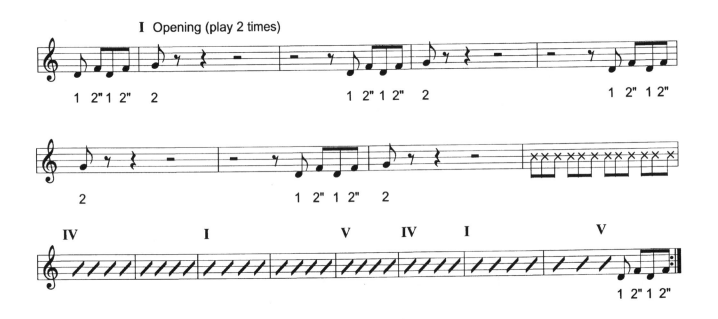

12 BAR JAM #8

<u>Key of Song</u>: A Minor   <u>Tempo</u>: 114   <u>Harmonica</u>: Lee Oskar A Natural Minor Harmonica in 2nd Position, G Major Harmonica in 3rd Position

<u>Song Description</u>: Medium-slow minor blues with break at turnaround   <u>Instrumentation</u>: Full band

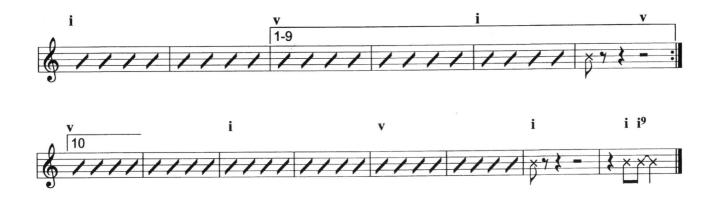

12 BAR JAM #9

Key of Song: G Major   Tempo: 176   Harmonica: C Harmonica in 2nd Position
Song Description: Fast shuffle with syncopation   Instrumentation: Full band

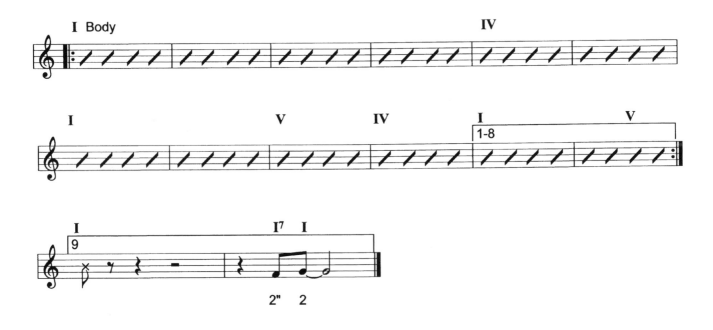